Snow Ponies

Snow Ponies

By CYNTHIA COTTEN

Illustrated by JASON COCKCROFT

SCHOLASTIC INC.

New York Toronto London Auckland Sydney
Mexico City New Delhi Hong Kong Buenos Aires

ISBN 0-439-49549-0

Text Copyright © 2001 by Cynthia Cotten.
Illustrations copyright © 2001 by Jason Cockcroft. All rights reserved.
Published by Scholastic Inc., 557 Broadway, New York, NY 10012,
by arrangement with Henry Holt and Company, LLC.
SCHOLASTIC and associated logos are trademarks and/or registered
trademarks of Scholastic Inc.

12 11 10 9 8 7 6 5 4 3 2   7 8 9/0

Printed in the U.S.A.   40

First Scholastic printing, November 2002

The artist used acrylic paint on paper to create
the illustrations for this book.

For Phyllis Root,
who helped me set these ponies free;
and for James Ashcraft, the first teacher
ever to make me rewrite something—
now I know why
—C. C.

To Ruth and Alan
—J. C.

On a cold, gray day, Old Man Winter walks out to his barn and opens the door.

"Hello, my pretty ones," he says. "It's a fine day for a romp." The snow ponies toss their heads and paw the floor.

One by one, he opens the stall doors and takes the snow ponies to a pen beside the barn. Soon the pen is full of ponies, jostling and prancing. Their breath makes white clouds that rise above their heads.

When all the ponies are in the pen, Old Man Winter walks among them, patting backs and rubbing noses.

"Are you ready?" he asks.
The ponies stamp their feet and shake their heads in reply.

Unfastening the gate, Old Man Winter
claps his hands. "Go on!" he calls.
And he leans against the fence and laughs
with delight.

The snow ponies flow out of the pen into the wide openness beyond the gate. Faster and faster they go, manes flying, tails streaming out behind them. Their feet make no sound on the cold, hard ground, and whatever they touch turns white.

The ponies are playful and full of energy. In a
flurry, they canter and call to each other. Their
whinnies and whickers whistle through the trees.

Little by little, they grow faster, louder. Creatures
of forest and field shiver and get out of their way.
The white-tailed deer waits in a woody thicket.

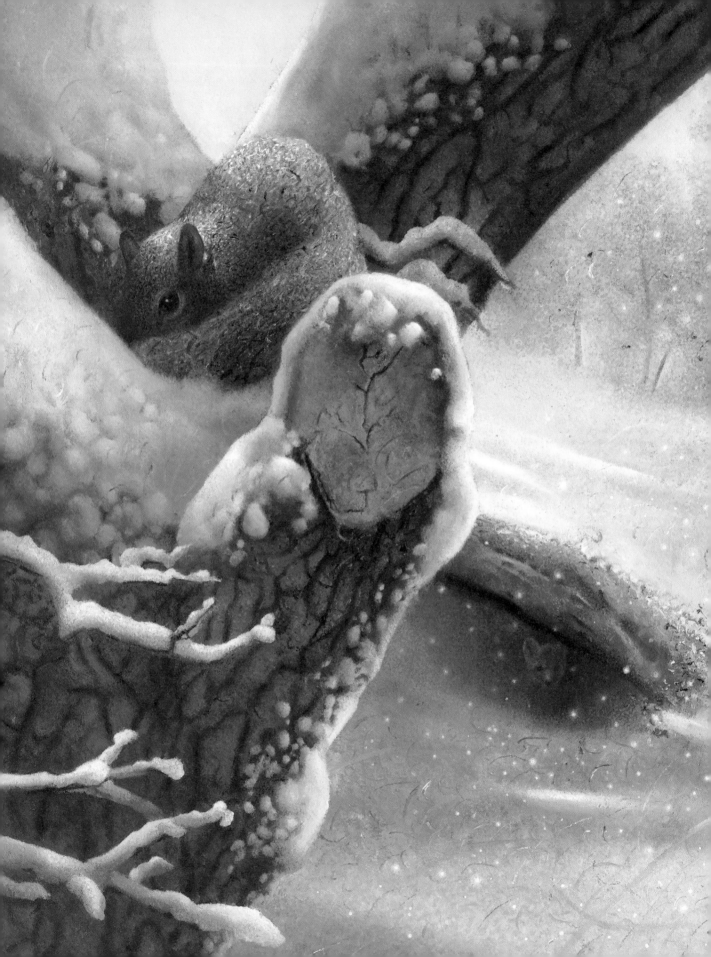

The gray squirrel curls up in the bare-branched oak.
The red fox snuggles in his cozy den.

And the songbird hides in the holly bush.
They watch and listen as the snow ponies frolic.

The ponies buck and rear and race. They spin and kick up their heels. Little clouds of snow whirl around them. Flakes fly off branches as they snort and blow. Wilder and wilder their play becomes. Through the woods and across the fields they gallop. They leap over fences and nip at each other's heels.

At last the snow ponies begin to tire. Back to the barn they drift, huddling together. Old Man Winter opens the door.

"Come, my pretty ones," he says. "Come and rest."

Back in their stalls the snow ponies shake their heads, shuffle their feet, and sigh long sleepy sighs. Old Man Winter rubs them down, covers them with blankets, and quietly shuts the door as he leaves.

The snow ponies close their eyes and slowly, slowly nod off to sleep.

Everything is white, as far as the eye can see.

And Old Man Winter smiles.